To Harper.

Our little mate.

Happy 4th birthday

love Pete & lynda

o x x

What Is A Secret Fairy Wish?

Written and illustrated by Kaye Anne

In loving memory of
my mum, Anne

Children from all around the world but especially in Whitstable in Kent and as far away as Mosley Hill in Merseyside, often wonder: 'What is a Secret Fairy Wish?'

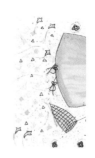

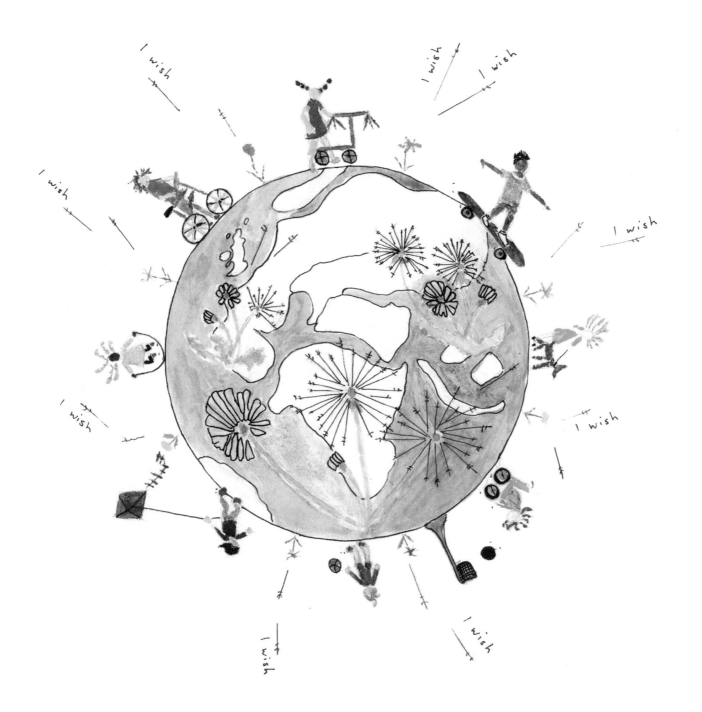

I used to dream about fairy wishes when I was a small child.

My mummy would read bed time stories to me about fairies
and their Magical Adventures.

I would have warm milk and a home-made cookie for my supper, and once I had eaten the last crumb and drank the last drop of milk, my mummy would tuck me up in bed and bounce me up and down under the quilt and say:

"As snug as a bug in a rug."

I would giggle and scream with delight saying: "One more, one more!" hoping to keep mummy with me for just a little longer.

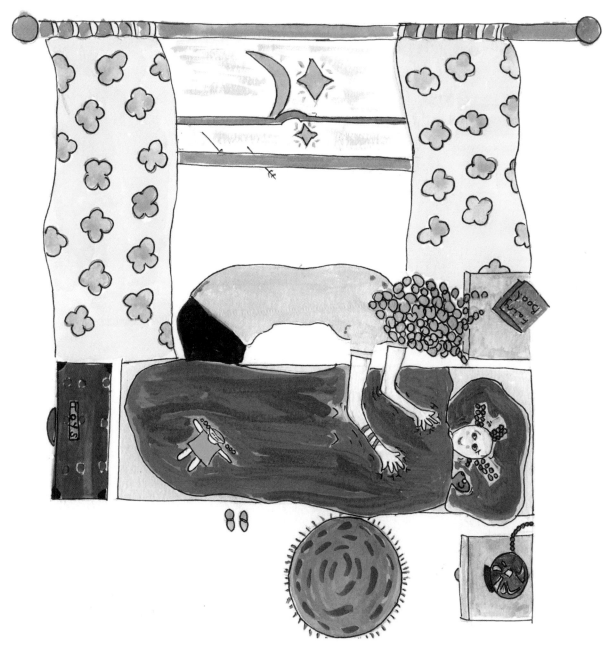

As snug as a bug in a rug

After more bouncing and being tucked in my bed for the very last time, my mummy would turn out the light saying with a smile and twinkly eyes: "Good night, sleep tight. Don't let the bed bugs bite. Sweet dreams. I love you and I'll see you in the morning."

My mummy would turn out the light

I would snuggle down further into my bed, and close my eyes.
Sometimes I could hear the wind blowing through the trees or
the sound of a distant train rumbling by or a dog barking or
beautiful music floating in through my window.

The sound of a distant train rumbling by

One very warm evening, the window was slightly open and I could hear something I'd not heard before. Out of the corner of my eye, I saw a flash of sparkling yellow light.

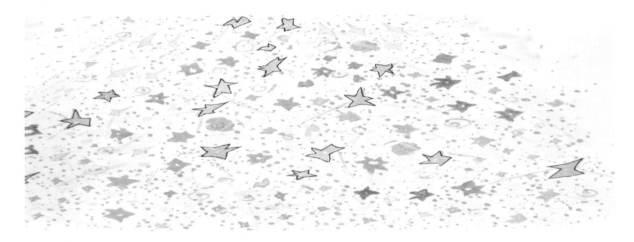

I blinked and blinked and rubbed my eyes until I could see the sparkling light hovering over me. It was a fairy!

She was wearing a bright yellow dress and, at the hem, two teeny tiny yellow boots were poking out.

It Was A Fairy!

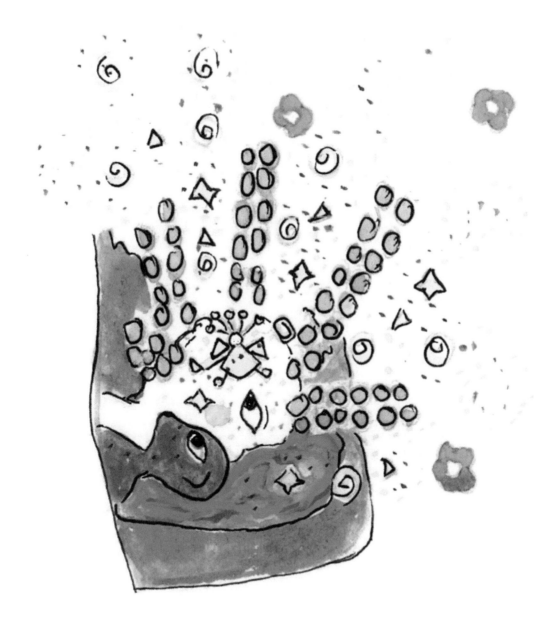

I wrinkled up my nose and thought:

"Why is she carrying a fishing net and not a wand?"

She didn't seem to mind as she was smiling and singing.

She landed on the nose of my teddy bear.

She landed on the nose of my teddy bear

Even though I could feel my heart pounding in my chest with excitement. I lay perfectly still.

The little fairy spoke to me with the sweetest and tiniest voice that I had ever heard. "Hello" she said. "I am Great Grandma Fairy Anne. Sorry to wake you but I am trying to catch secret fairy wishes and I followed one in through your bedroom window.

Great Grandma Fairy Anne

"A secret Fairy wish? WOW! What is a secret Fairy Wish?" I asked.

Great Grandma Fairy Anne smiled and said "A secret fairy wish begins with a dandelion hunt in your garden or if you don't have a garden, you can look for them in the park when you're out with your mummy and daddy or with grandma and grandpa or your brothers and sisters, aunties and uncles, cousins and friends.

It's a great game you can all play together."

The dandelion hunt

"What is a dandelion?"

I asked.

"Dandelions are beautiful yellow flowers," explained Great Grandma Fairy Anne. "The real magic begins when the yellow flowers turn into round balls of silver fluff. This is the dandelion fruit. Some children and grown ups call them dandelion clocks but they have many other names around the world."

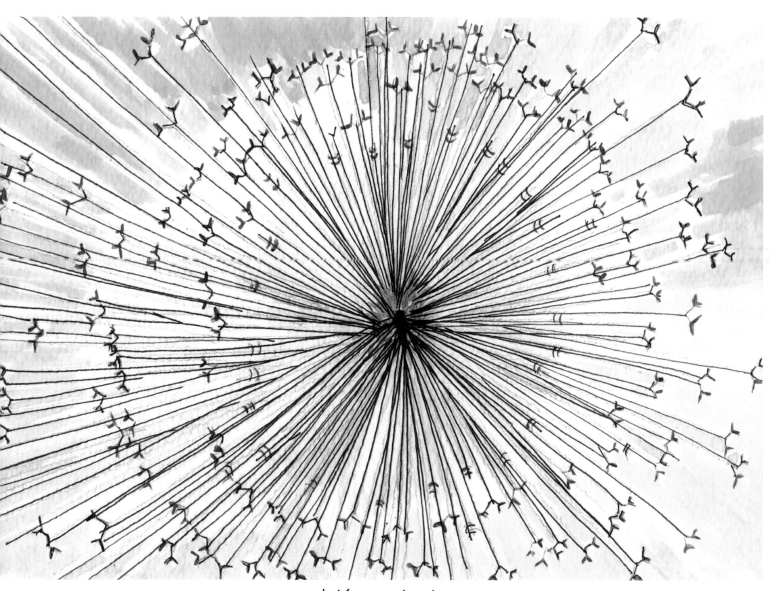

Dandelion Clock

"A Secret Fairy Wish doesn't just happen. It has to be helped along by you."

"What do I have to do?" I asked.

"You begin by picking a dandelion clock and gently holding it in your hand."

Great Grandma Fairy Anne chuckled, as she saw my eyes growing wider and my mouth opening in amazement.

"Next, you must squeeze your eyes shut tight and whisper your secret wish. But be sure that there is no one around to hear it."

"I won't, I promise," I said.

"...you must squeeze your eyes shut tight and whisper your secret wish."

"When you have made your fairy wish," said Grandma Fairy Anne. "You take a deep breath and blow the dandelion clock as hard as you can – just as if you were blowing out the candles on a birthday cake. Sometimes you have to blow and blow to send your secret wish on its way."

"Then what happens?" I asked.

Tra-ling!

Great Grandma Fairy Ann sang: "Tra-ling, Tra-ling."

"Tra-ling, Tra-ling" I sang.

Great Grandma Fairy Anne hovered above teddy's nose with excitement. Her little boots floating and bobbing up and down.

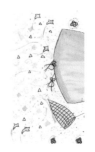

"And with the help of my fairy family, we begin catching the secret fairy wishes with our magic nets."

"So that's why you have little nets!" I said.

Great Grandma Fairy Anne whizzed around teddy's head as she swished her little net. "That's right," she said.

"We then join hands to make a fairy circle and sing our magic song:"

You are a secret fairy wish, floating in the breeze,

We spin around, float up and down,

And whirl around the trees.

We dance and sing: tra-ling tra-ling,

We also touch our noses.

To make your fairy wish come true

We also touch our toes-es.

"We then join hands to make a fairy circle and sing our magic song"

"You can see how important teamwork is in order to make your fairy wish come true," said Great Grandma Fairy Anne.

"Secret Fairy Wishes that float past the fairy catcher nets have a very important job too. They will grow into new Dandelion flowers to make new wishes in the gardens and parks near you."

Teddy and I then saw a flash of yellow light full of magic fairy dust disappear out of the open window and into the night sky.

Yawning, I closed my eyes as I heard Grandma Fairy Anne giggle and sing:

You are a secret fairy wish, floating in the breeze,

We spin around, float up and down,

And whirl around the trees.

We dance and sing: tra-ling tra-ling,

We also touch our noses,

To make your fairy wish come true,

We also touch our toes-es.

"Good night, sleep tight. Don't let the bed bugs bite.

Sweet dreams little girl. Until the next time."

THE END

Printed in Great Britain
by Amazon